KT-524-368

DOODLEBUG
SUMMER

DOODLEBUG SUMMER

ALISON PRINCE

A & C Black • London

First published 2006 by
A & C Black Publishers Ltd
38 Soho Square, London, W1D 3HB

www.acblack.com

ISBN 0-7136-7579-9
ISBN 978-0-713-67579-5

A CIP catalogue for this book is available from the British Library.

A & C Black uses paper produced with elemental chlorine-free
pulp, harvested from managed sustained forests.

Printed and bound in Great Britain by Bookmarque Ltd, Croydon

Contents

1

Pauline and Me

'It's such a good tree,' Pauline says.

'Yes. Lovely.' We both know how we feel about it – words aren't needed, really.

It's almost three years since our tree nearly got destroyed, but we still have these moments of feeling glad it's here.

I'm above her, sitting astride the big branch that sticks out sideways. Pauline's in the place where the main trunk divides. She doesn't like being higher up, she says there's too much air under her feet. I don't mind. It's like being on a big horse, riding through the sky.

I can see the bomb crater over the top of the bushes from where I am, it's near the barbed-wire encampment where the anti-aircraft guns are. There's water at the bottom of the crater now, and brambles are growing round the edge. It isn't the only one. A whole stick of bombs fell on the common that night, but this is the one that nearly got our tree. We didn't know until we came up a day or two later. Most of its smaller branches had been blown off and it looked an awful mess, but it was still standing.

The air raids stopped soon after that. Nights went by, and the sirens didn't sound. We went on sleeping in the shelter in our garden for quite a while, then Mum said she thought we could come back indoors. It's been great to sleep in my own bed, with a proper bedside light instead of a Hurricane oil lamp hanging on the concrete wall and casting weird shadows.

'We had a letter from my dad this morning,' Pauline says.

'Did you? Is he OK?'

Her dad is away in the Army.

'Yes, he's fine. He says the war will be over soon – he reckons we've got them on the run.' She means the Germans, of course. Pauline always sounds very tough, like her dad.

He used to work in the garage on the corner of our road until he got called up. I remember him as a thin man in a navy boiler suit, with red hair like Pauline's only cut so short that you wouldn't know it was curly.

I wonder if he's right about the war ending. I was six when it began, and I'm eleven now. Looking back to when I was small, everything seems full of sunshine and ice creams, though perhaps I'm just remembering the good bits. The streets used to be lit up at night and we didn't have to pull blackout curtains across our windows. The shops were full of things to buy if you had the money. Now, most of them are boarded up because of bomb blast, and there's nothing in them anyway except the rationed stuff: meat, cheese, sugar, margarine. One packet of butter a week, to share between four of us. Mum divides it up into four dishes, otherwise my brother Ian says it's not fair.

'Dad thinks he might be home by Christmas,' Pauline goes on. 'But Mum says we mustn't count our chickens.'

Pauline's mum is skinny, too, like her husband. She works in a munitions factory, putting explosive into shell-cases, so Pauline and her big sister Chrissie look after the two younger ones a lot of the time. It's a bit of a squeeze in their small house, and there's no indoor toilet – you have to go across the yard. Lots of houses are like that.

We're lucky really. Our house was built just before the war, and it's got a bathroom and toilet upstairs and another little toilet outside by the coal shed. And there are three bedrooms, so I don't have to share with Ian. He's not five yet, but he's fussy about the way his stuff is arranged. He hates it if you move anything. I leave things all over the place, and he thinks that's awful. We'd drive each other up the wall if we shared a room.

'Katie,' says Pauline, 'have you done your homework yet?'

'Course not.'

I know what she's going to ask.

'Can I come round to yours and we'll do it together? It's just the French, really.'

I try not to sigh. 'OK,' I say.

Pauline hates French. She's good at maths, though, and I'm rubbish, so I suppose it's a fair swap. But that means we'll have to spend tomorrow afternoon doing homework. I usually leave it until Sunday night, but Pauline can't come round in the evening. None of us go out after dark on our own. Even though it's been quiet for so long, you still never know if there might be a raid.

'Thanks ever so much,' Pauline says. 'About half-past two?'

'Fine.'

She's climbing out of the tree. 'Got to go,' she says. 'Mum's on early shift, and Chrissie's going to the pictures with May. I said I'd look after the little ones.'

She's like a grown-up in some ways, getting on with whatever has to be done. I think I'd grumble about it, but she never seems to mind.

Hedge has come to do the garden. I always know when he's here. The smell of him reaches me as soon as I come round the side of the house. It's a mixture of earth and tobacco and dog – and of Hedge, who looks as if he never washes.

Dad calls him 'Hedge'. Mum says I must call him *Mr* Hedge, but somehow I can't do that. I don't call him anything.

His dog is here today, lying in the covered bit between the back door and the coal shed, on the jacket Hedge has taken off.

'Hello, Kelly,' I say, but he doesn't wag his tail or even raise his head from his paws, just looks up at me with his yellow eyes. He's a big dog, brown and rough. I don't know what sort he is. Dad says he's like liquorice. All sorts.

I go carefully past Kelly, into the kitchen.

'There you are,' Mum says. 'That's good. Run out and tell him his tea's ready, will you?'

She doesn't call Hedge anything, either.

I skirt past Kelly again and walk across the lawn.

Ian is counting the flowers on the marigolds. 'Two hundred and eighty-one,' he says.

'Is that good?'

'Seventeen more than yesterday. But I haven't finished yet.'

I don't know how he does this numbers thing. I just think of marigolds as orange – I've no idea how many of them there are.

Mum flaps a hand at me through the window. *Go on*, she means. *Tell him*. So I go on, over the bit of grass where we hang the washing and past the steps that lead down to our underground air-raid shelter between the fruit trees. It'll be horrible in there after all this time of not using it, damp and musty. It's probably growing toadstools.

Hedge is squashing caterpillars on the gooseberry bushes. The creepies are striped black and yellow, and his fingers are all mucky with them. His sleeves are rolled up, and his brown arms are crisscrossed with blood-dotted scratches. He must have been pruning the roses that ramble over the fence – he never seems to mind their thorns.

He looks up and says, 'Tea time, is it?'

'Yes.'

'Tha's good.'

He picks off a final caterpillar, crushes it and wipes his finger and thumb on his trousers, then sets off towards the house.

I walk beside him. I can't help looking at the scratches on his arm.

'Don't they hurt?' I ask.

He glances at them. 'No,' he says, and laughs in a spitty kind of way because his teeth are all broken and gappy. 'Them's all right.'

Mum has put two big hunks of bread and cheese on a plate in the place where he sits, and a mug of tea. She's given up asking if he wants to wash his hands, he never does. I don't know how she can spare the cheese from the ration, but she manages somehow. Hedge keeps hens, so he brings her some eggs sometimes, and lots of things like carrots and leeks and beetroot. It's a big help. There's never much in the shops.

It's funny how you have to keep watching someone even if they give you the shudders. I can't help watching Hedge. He cuts the cheese up with a heavy old clasp knife he takes out of his pocket, and puts a chunk of it into his mouth with a lump of bread. He talks as he's munching, and splutters crumbs through his dreadful teeth.

'You bin plantin' things again,' he says to Mum, as if it's a crime.

She turns a bit pink and says, 'Mrs Potter gave me these sweet-pea seedlings, so I thought I'd better get them in.'

He shakes his head. 'You can't be plantin' now, not when the moon's goin' down. You need to catch her when she's risin'. Tha's when things grow.'

'Oh, I see,' Mum says. 'Sorry.'

'Nuther time, you just leave 'em to me.'

'Yes, perhaps I'd better.'

My dad isn't a bit like Hedge. He plays the piano, and when we go to the library, he borrows old, dusty books that nobody else would bother with. He's hopeless about gardening. He saw some flowers growing by the coal shed once and said, 'Those are nice,' and Mum said, 'They're dandelions.' I quite like dandelions, really.

Mum shouts through the window to Ian, 'Do you want some milk and biscuits?'

'No!' he shouts back. 'Three hundred and ten.'

He goes on counting. I can't imagine how he got to be so good at numbers when he's so young. But then, I can't imagine why Pauline has such a struggle with French.

2

The Start of It

Madame Souris a une maison. *Mrs Mouse has a house.*

Pauline and I are in a house. It's underground, so there aren't any windows, but there are gold medals all over its walls, in between framed oil paintings of mice. We won the medals because we're very good at French.

'What a dreadful noise,' says Mrs Mouse, frowning at us as she wipes her paws on her apron. 'It'll be a tractor. That's the trouble when you let humans in, they bring their machinery with them.'

I was going to tell her I don't have a tractor, but then I woke up. Madame Souris was right, there *is* a noise. It's not a tractor, though. It sounds more like a motorbike, but louder, with an engine that's not working very well. It's coming closer.

Du-du-du-du-du-du-du-du-DU-DU-DU – Good, it's stopped. Turn over, go back to sleep again.

BANG!

The explosion shakes me in my bed.

That's *heavy*, I think. I'm used to bombs, I know the difference between the high-explosive ones and the lighter firebombs, but this is something new. The crash was incredibly loud, and I've never heard anything like the stuttering engine sound. And if there's a raid on, why haven't we heard the air-raid siren? Why aren't the guns firing?

Ian's woken up, he's crying. I switch my light on. I can hear Mum getting out of bed. Dad's not here, he's on fire-watch duty at the bank in London where he works. All the staff have to take a turn, and this weekend it's him.

The motorbike noise is starting again.

It's very scary. I pull the bedclothes over my head and curl up like a caterpillar, though I know it's useless. It takes more than an eiderdown to keep you safe, but having something close and warm round you makes you feel better.

The noise is coming closer – *du-du-du-du-du-DU* – it's stopped.

BANG!

The explosion comes at once this time, and even louder.

Mum opens the door. She's in her dressing gown, and Ian's beside her, clutching his old bit of blanket and Bun, this rather bald rabbit that he has to have at night.

'Katie, love, we'd better get downstairs,' Mum says.

'What was it?'

Stupid question – she can't know.

'Could have been a damaged aeroplane that crashed. Only I can't see why there should be two. Come on, quickly.'

The noise is starting up again.

'Bring something warm,' she calls back from the landing.

I know the drill, we've rushed for the shelter often enough in the night raids. I grab my dressing gown, push my feet into my slippers, gather up my eiderdown, and stumble down the stairs after Mum. The noise gets louder and I grab the banister in case an explosion should throw me off my feet, but the thing passes overhead and goes on. When the bang comes, it's a more distant one, and I'm standing safely in the hall. Mum's pulling things out of the cupboard under the stairs, a bit hampered by Ian, who is clinging to her dressing gown and getting in the way.

I take his hand and say, 'Where's Bun? Oh, you've got him safe. That's good.'

'We can't go out to the shelter,' Mum says to me over her shoulder. 'It'll be in an awful state, unused for so long, and anyway—'

I know what she means. It's too dangerous to go out across the garden.

'This'll be fun,' I tell Ian. 'We'll get in the cupboard and pretend it's a stable. We'll be horses.'

'Why?'

'Because that's where horses sleep. In stables.'

He frowns, but he's interested. 'What are their names?'

'I don't know. Think of something nice.'

'Dan,' he says.

'That's a good name.'

'How many horses are there?'

'Two.'

'That's not enough.'

'OK, we'll have more. How many would you like?'

'Seventy-three,' he says.

Mum's handing stuff out to me: the vacuum cleaner, the ironing board, flowerpots with dead hyacinth bulbs in them. I stack them against the wall. The noise is starting again.

'In, quickly,' she says. 'There's another one coming.'

Ian starts to cry again. We bundle into the cupboard and I sit on the shoe-cleaning box, hugging him tightly. Mum pulls the door shut. It's pitch black, and Ian wails louder.

There's another heavy explosion, but not terribly close.

Mum's listening. Everything seems quiet, so she opens the door again. A bit of light comes in from the hall, but the depths of the cupboard are still dark.

'You've got your horse rug,' I say to Ian. 'That's good.'

He's not in a mood for pretending. 'It isn't a horse rug. It's my blanket.' He rubs his tear-wet face with Bun. That rabbit gets in a dreadful state, but he hates Mum washing it.

I keep going with the horse game.

'This is our stable,' I tell him. 'I'm Black Beauty.' I do a whinny. 'Hello, Dan, it's good in here, isn't it.'

'Don't want to be Dan.'

'Be a pony, then. Be Merrilegs.' I've been reading *Black Beauty* for the umpteenth time. It's terribly sad, but somehow I have to keep reading it.

'Don't want to be a pony.'

'What about an elephant?'

He ignores that. 'Switch the light on,' he says, instead.

'There isn't a light in here,' says Mum. 'I'll go and find a torch. Stay where you are.'

The cupboard smells of furniture polish and old rags. Ian is shivering a bit. He's heavy on my lap, and the edge of the shoe-cleaning box is cutting into my legs, but it's all right. This is my job to do, looking after my little brother. I can see why Pauline doesn't mind being in charge of the little ones. It makes you feel better if someone's depending on you.

Mum comes back with an armful of rugs and blankets, and two pillows.

'Where's the torch?' asks Ian.

'You can have it in a minute,' she says. 'Katie, hand me out some more stuff, see if you can make space to lie down. Oh, hang on, there's another one coming.' She crouches down beside us, and pulls the door to again.

The stuttering engine is getting louder. Our own guns have got going as well, with a barrage of sharp bangs.

Ian clutches me and says, 'I don't like it!'

I jiggle him on my knee and say, 'Never mind.'

It's funny how you can't go on being very frightened for too long. After a bit you just settle into waiting for it to end.

It's difficult to tell if the thing has exploded yet, because of the racket from the guns, but it's gone over, anyway. Mum goes on moving things to make space. I shift further in with Ian.

'Mind your head,' I tell him, 'the ceiling slopes.'

'I *know*.' He sounds irritated. 'We're underneath the stairs, so it has to.'

'I'll get the cushions off the sofa,' Mum says. 'They'll make a bed.'

Ian grabs at her. 'Mummy, don't keep going out. Stay *here*.'

'I'll only be a minute.' She's out in the hall again.

'We're going to have oats and hay,' I tell him.

Mistake. He thumps me on the chest and says, 'I don't *want* to be a horse.'

'OK. Tell you what, we'll have a midnight picnic.'

'Picnics are outside.'

'Not always, you can have them anywhere.'

That cheers him up a bit. 'With sandwiches?'

'If you like.'

'Jam sandwiches.'

'Right.'

That's a relief, I thought he might want something impossible like eggs.

Hedge hasn't brought any for a while, and there are none in the shops.

'Here,' says Mum, handing in the big cushions off the sofa, 'wedge these side by side.'

I start wedging. 'Ian's hungry. Can I make some sandwiches?'

'I'll make them, you stay where you are.'

She crouches down beside us because there's another one coming. The gunfire had stopped, but it opens up again.

Mum says, 'These things are going towards London.'

Dad's in London. I almost ask if she can ring him up, but that's silly. The switchboard won't be working at this time of night. Everyone's gone home except the two who are on fire-watch.

She hands me the torch. 'Don't use it unless you have to, the batteries are almost gone. There are none in the shops. I'll make the sandwiches.'

'Jam sandwiches,' says Ian. 'I want *jam* sandwiches.'

Once he's got an idea in his head, he doesn't let go.

Will this night never end? I'm aching with tiredness but I can't imagine dozing off while all this scary noise is going on. Ian's asleep, thank goodness. I felt him jump when the biggest explosion came, and he muttered something but he didn't wake. I'm glad, because it was very close. The house shook and the light in the hall went out.

Mum took the torch and went to see if we'd been damaged, and when she came back she said the upstairs windows have been blown in. And the electricity is off.

The cupboard door is open. Mum's stopped diving in every time one of the things comes over. She put her daytime clothes on while Ian and I were eating the sandwiches, and now she's standing in the kitchen with a tin hat on, staring through the window. She's drawn the curtains back a bit – no need to worry about the blackout, since we can't put any lights on anyway. I can see her silhouetted against the flashes of gunfire. She's knitting as she stands there, with the ball of wool in her coat pocket. She's a good knitter, she never needs to look at what her hands are doing.

She's coming over to the cupboard.

'You awake?' she whispers.

'Yes.'

'You want to see what these things look like?'

I nod and start to scramble up, being careful not to disturb Ian.

'Don't come right out, just stand at the cupboard door.'

We watch together. Among the flashes of gunfire, a purposeful streak of orange light is heading towards us with the sound we've started to get used to: *du-du-du-du-du*. Whatever the thing is, it has a tail of flame. It passes overhead, and the noise is thunderous.

It's stopped.

Mum and I dive into the cupboard and pull the door shut behind us. It's quite a long wait for the bang this time, and when it comes, it's distant, though still heavier than the sound of the guns.

'Someone else,' says Mum. 'Poor souls.'

No need to ask what she means. Someone else's house destroyed, someone else killed or hurt. Not us. Not this time, thank the Lord. We never say much about it. If we got upset, it would make everything much worse.

Mum goes back to the kitchen. She's still knitting.

I wake feeling cramped and stiff. My arm's gone numb because Ian's head is resting across it. Outside, the dawn is getting paler.

Mum's opening the back door. The guns have stopped, but there's a quiet rattling sound, very close to the house. It could be dangerous. Surely she can't be going out?

She laughs. What on earth is she laughing at?

I creep out and join her.

'What is it?'

'Look!' she whispers.

There's a hedgehog by the doorstep. It's got its nose stuck in a golden syrup tin. Syrup's not rationed, so we get it whenever we can, and a hedgehog often comes to lick the empty tin. But this one's jammed himself in. He's blundering about with the can over his head, bumping into things.

Mum and I are falling about with laughter, hands over our mouths in case we wake Ian.

'I heard all this clattering – I thought it was another secret weapon,' Mum says.

Gently, she pulls the tin off the hedgehog's bristles, and after a rather puzzled pause, it shuffles off round the corner to the garden.

'Glass of milk and a biscuit?' Mum asks.

I shake my head.

'Tired?'

'Not really.'

I know I won't go back to sleep again, but there's nothing else to do. I crawl back in beside Ian. It's not exactly comfortable, but it's warm. And out there, everything is quiet…

3

Rockets

I'm awake again. There are voices in the
kitchen. It's Mrs Potter from next door,
talking to Mum.

'Ted says he reckons they're rockets,' she's
saying. 'Inhuman, I call it. I mean, what can
you do against rockets? They don't give you
a chance.'

Ian's sitting at the table, eating cornflakes.
He looks pretty normal, but I feel stiff and
tired and grubby. I'm still in my pyjamas
and dressing gown.

'They say there's a terrible mess up by Park
Road,' Mrs Potter goes on. 'Two people
were killed.'

'Yes, I know.' Mum gives her a tiny shake
of the head, warning her not to go on about

it in front of Ian. She turns to him and asks, 'Have you finished your breakfast?'

He nods and gets down from the table. 'I'm going to look for shrapnel in the garden,' he says. He always used to do that after the night raids. 'I've got twenty-three bits.'

He fishes the tin bowl out from under the sink and shows Mrs Potter his collection of jagged metal fragments. They're shell-bursts from our guns mostly, red-hot when they come down, but they're rusty now. Those ordinary raids seem quite cosy compared with the weirdness of the night that's just gone.

'This is the best one,' Ian says, holding up the biggest chunk. 'Look, you can see the grooves. Dad says they put those on the shells to make them twist, so they keep in a straight line.'

Dad. A worry jumps back into my mind.

'Did you phone Dad?' I ask Mum. 'Is he all right?'

'The phone lines are down,' she says.

Ian goes to the back door and opens it.

'If you're going out, stay in the back garden,' Mum warns. 'Don't go round the front. And if you find anything unusual, don't touch it.'

He looks at her pityingly. 'Of course not.' He turns at the door, suddenly doubtful. 'There aren't any more of those things coming, are there?'

Mum and Mrs Potter glance at each other, but only for a moment.

'No, it's all quiet just now,' Mum says. 'But if you hear one coming, run in here, quickly.'

He nods. He stands at the door for another few moments, then he closes it and comes back to the table. 'I think I'll stay here,' he says.

'All right,' says Mum, not making any fuss about it. 'Katie, I put clean clothes for you next door in the dining room. Be careful where you tread. All the upstairs windows have gone, and there's broken glass all over the place.'

The kitchen light suddenly comes on.

'That's the electricity back,' says Mrs Potter. 'Try the radio – there might be some news.'

Mum switches on the radio, but it's just playing music.

It seems funny, getting dressed in the dining room. I almost pull the curtains across in case Hedge is out there watching me, but it's all right, this isn't the morning when he comes. I've got my slippers on, but Mum's put my school shoes out, I suppose because of the glass. I put them on and lace them up.

In the hall, it seems lighter than usual. There's a wind blowing down from the top of the stairs. I want to see what's happened up there.

The stair carpet is crunchy under my feet because the window at the top of the stairs has blown in. There's a lot more glass on the landing, mixed with flat bits of white plaster where a patch of the ceiling has fallen down. It'll be a huge job to get it all cleared up.

The door of my room is standing open. I don't have to go in to see that my curtains are hanging in tatters, wafting a bit in the breeze that's coming through the empty windows. There's glass all over my bed. How long will it be before we sleep in our beds again? I suppose we'll have to go back to the air-raid shelter now these new things have started coming.

It's even worse in Mum and Dad's room. The window frames have been smashed as well as all the glass, and the broken remains stick up in splinters, no more use than firewood. I can see through to the houses opposite. They're worse than ours. The roofs are sagging and broken, and the one on the left where the Greens live has lost half its corner wall. How stupid we were to think the war was almost over.

Back in the kitchen, they're listening to the news. The announcer is droning on about our successful raids on Germany last night. Now he's switched to a story about a man who won a Dig For Victory competition with a giant marrow.

'Oh, come *on*,' says Mrs Potter.

'There was slight enemy activity over southern England last night,' he says. 'And now for the weather forecast.'

'*Slight*?' says Mum. 'What does he mean, *slight*?'

She and I and Mrs Potter are laughing and groaning because this is so stupid, but Ian says, 'How much is slight?'

'Almost nothing,' says Mum.

The back door opens. Dad comes in.

Mum jumps up to hug him. 'Oh, thank goodness,' she says. 'Are you all right?'

'A bit tired,' says Dad. 'Been up all night.'

'We've been up, too,' says Ian, though he was asleep most of the time.

Dad ruffles his hair and says, 'I'm sure you have.' He hangs his coat up and sits down at the kitchen table.

'Is there much damage in London?' Mrs Potter asks.

'A fair bit,' says Dad. 'One of these things fell behind the building across the road from us. I think the suburbs are worse, though, from what I saw on the train. Catford caught a fair old packet.'

'Dreadful,' says Mrs Potter. She gets up from the table and sighs. 'Well, better go and peel some spuds, I suppose – I'll have Ted home for his lunch. Business as usual, eh?'

Nobody smiles. It's been chalked on bombed shops for years.

That was two weeks ago. We know what the things are now. Doodlebugs, people call them. Flying bombs. They come over more by day than by night, so we can see them. They're like stubby little aeroplanes, only they don't have a pilot. They're packed with explosive, and they work on a rocket motor that stops when it runs out of fuel. Sometimes they nose-dive and blow up at once, other times they glide for a long way, you never know.

All the schools are closed for the time being. And we're into the summer holidays now, so they won't open again until September. Mum won't let me go and meet Pauline, she says it's too dangerous for us to be out on our own. I don't even go round to the shops with her, because Ian's scared to go out and I have to stay and look after him. It's the same for Pauline – she's stuck in the house or the air-raid shelter with the little ones.

There's a weird kind of excitement about the doodlebugs. We never know when they're going to arrive. It's not like the old raids when the siren went to warn that planes were coming, then sounded the All Clear when it was safe again. It's never safe now. These things are being fired from the coast of Holland, where the Germans occupy the country, and they get here so fast, there's no chance of any warning.

Dad goes to work as usual. He says life has to go on. I don't like him being away in London, I'd rather we were all together. Leaving us each day is probably worse for him, though. Everyone knows most of the doodlebugs explode south of London, before they get as far as the centre.

They're difficult to shoot down because they go so fast, but anti-aircraft guns wouldn't be much good anyway. The rockets explode when they hit the ground, so shooting them down in built-up areas wouldn't be a good idea.

It says on the news that our barrage balloons are catching them before they get to the city, but Mrs Potter's husband says they hardly ever get one. He's on a barrage balloon site, down in Kent, so he knows what's going on. The balloons float in the sky on long cables, and if a doodlebug catches its wing on them, it'll crash straight away instead of flying on to the city. But the balloons aren't very close together, so most of the bombs get through.

Our fighter planes have started going after them. I love watching when they do that, it's really exciting. If a pilot can catch up with one, he comes alongside it, both of them flying at terrific speed, and gets his wing tip exactly under the wing of the doodlebug. Then he tilts his plane and flips the thing sideways, and it goes bumbling off in a new direction, away from London. It's a dangerous game, because if he gets it wrong the bomb will blow up. It often works, though, and it makes you feel like cheering when it does.

Ian gets in a panic when I stand in the garden and watch what's happening in the sky, even though I wear a tin hat. He doesn't have to worry. If a doodlebug's engine cuts out, there's time to run for the shelter, but he stands at the top of its steps, screaming at me to hurry.

The War Damage repair people mended our windows, but they've used thick wartime glass that you can't see through properly. It just about lets the light in, but the front bedrooms look greenish, as if you're in a dirty fish-tank. Not that it matters – we don't go upstairs much now – we've got a Morrison.

That's an indoor shelter like a big table made of solid steel. Mum and I hauled the mattresses down from upstairs and pushed them inside, wedged with some cushions, then tucked sheets over it all as best we could. It's not quite like a real bed, but the four of us can sleep there side by side. It's more crowded than the shelter in the garden was, but we can't sleep in that because the canvas of the bunks has rotted away in the damp. Morrisons are supposed to protect you from being crushed under the wreckage if the house gets blown up. I think it's a good idea – much handier than having to rush out across the garden, though we do nip into the outside shelter during the day if we happen to be out of doors.

Dad hates the Morrison – he says it makes him feel as if he's shut in a box. That's rubbish, of course – it's a steel table with open sides, so it's not dark or anything. But it's less than waist-high to an adult, so you can only get in by crawling, so I suppose he feels a bit cramped.

Ian loves it, though. He spends quite a lot of time in there with his blanket and Bun. He's got a passion for doing jigsaws at the moment. They're the wooden sort, with quite big bits. He's supposed to put them away before we go to bed, but he doesn't always manage it.

'For goodness' sake, boy,' Dad said when he tucked him in one night, 'this bed's like a timberyard.'

Ian laughed a lot. He's got a weird sense of humour. He kept saying, 'Timberyard, timberyard,' as if it was a kind of poem.

I had a weird moment this evening. I was out in the garden, gathering plums that the wasps hadn't got at. Everything was quiet and the sun was going down behind the trees. I could hear Dad playing the piano. He always plays after tea, for hours sometimes. I've grown up with his music so I don't usually take much notice, but this time I heard it in a new way. It was very wistful and beautiful, something by Chopin I think, and it made me want to cry. I've never cried about the war, not even the time little Moira Blake was killed when their flat over the chemist's shop was hit. I just thought, *No, I mustn't give in.* But standing in the garden with the evening smell of the grass and the slow, lovely music, I suddenly felt the pity of it all, and tears came.

Mrs Potter's cat had kittens yesterday. I wanted to go and look at them, but Mum wouldn't let me. There were six, but Mr Potter said that was too many. He took four of them up to Hedge's cottage to be 'dealt with'. I know what that means. Hedge will drown them. I think that's really horrible. Poor little things. I hate Hedge.

We're back at school now. They sent a letter saying we'd lost so much time at the end of last term due to 'enemy activity', we really had to get back to work.

Mrs Potter's in the kitchen again. She's always popping in. Mum gets a bit fed up with it sometimes.

They both look up as I come in, and their faces are grave. There's something wrong.

'Katie,' Mum says, reaching out an arm for me. 'Something very sad has happened. You know Mr Freeman?'

I nod. He's a carpenter. He came here to put up some shelves for Dad's books, and got a splinter in his thumb. Mum sat him down at the kitchen table and took it out for him with a needle.

'He was killed yesterday, in that big explosion. He lived over on the estate. That's where it fell.'

'Oh, no!' I can see him so clearly, sitting at this table where Mrs Potter is now.

'Sunday, you see,' says Mrs Potter. 'He was at home, playing football in the garden with his two little boys.'

'Billy and Martin,' I hear myself say. Billy is at my school. Martin's too small to go to school yet.

Mrs Potter is rattling on. 'They heard a doodlebug coming and ran to their shelter, only Martin tripped and fell. Mr Freeman stopped to help him up.' She shakes her head. 'It was one of the sort that didn't glide...'

Yes, I know. We all heard it.

'Is Martin—' I can't ask.

'He's all right,' Mum says. 'He was injured, but the hospital says he'll be OK.'

'What about their mum?'

'She'd gone to see her sister.'

'That's good, isn't it. At least the boys have got their mother.'

It's the sort of thing you have to say, but it doesn't help a lot. Last time Mr Freeman was here, he drew a picture of a battleship on a spare bit of wood and gave it to Ian. He used to whistle through his teeth while he worked. The tip of his little finger was missing because of an accident with a circular saw, and he said he never even felt it when it happened.

I'm going to think about him sawing wood and whistling, I'm not going to think about their garden after the doodlebug fell, there's no point, it won't make anything better.

'His poor wife,' says Mrs Potter.

Why doesn't she shut up?

I break away from Mum and pull the back door open. Out in the garden I rage at the sun in the blue sky, furious with God, or fate or whatever it is. Why should a nice man like Mr Freeman be killed when horrible people like Hedge are walking around, perfectly OK? It's not fair. If I could choose, Hedge would have died instead. I run all the way to the back fence where the poplar trees used to grow, and thump my clenched fists against its splintery wood because I am so angry.

4

What Now?

I love the swing in our garden, especially on a warm, sunny day like this. Dad got Hedge to rig it up as a present for Ian's birthday, but Ian doesn't like it much, he says it makes him feel wobbly. I'm too big for it really, I have to hold my feet out in front so they don't catch on the grass, but I don't mind. The ropes are good and long, and when I get it swinging really high, I lean back with my arms and legs straight, and the plum tree leaves and bright bits of sky zoom one way and the other until I'm almost dizzy. Then the rocking slows down until I work it up again. This summer, with nothing much else to do except watch out for the flying bombs, I've spent ages just swinging. Today's a Saturday and I'm home from school, so that's what I'm doing right now, gently rocking to and fro.

It's September now, but the autumn days are still lovely. For some weeks, the sky's been strangely quiet and empty except for birds flying and twittering. The doodlebugs have stopped coming. When Hedge was here on Saturday he said the workers who have to build them in Holland are mucking them up so they don't work any more.

I was going to ask how he knew that, but Mum nodded and said, 'Sabotage. It's very brave of them, isn't it. If they were caught doing it, they'd be shot.'

I'm glad I don't live in Holland. The war's no fun here, but at least the Germans haven't marched into our country and occupied it. It would be awful to have them walking around in those uniforms with swastikas on the sleeves, shooting people who don't do as they're told.

Mum's not sure the doodlebugs really have stopped. She still won't let me go out of the house alone, and it's no use hoping I can go and meet Pauline. I can see how she feels,

I suppose. There's nowhere to shelter on the common. We'd be out in the open if anything happened.

I wonder if our tree's all right. Hedge says there's a big, new crater on the common where a doodlebug blew up three weeks ago, and he'll know because he lives near there. I'm not going to ask him about the tree, though. He'd never understand, even if I could explain which one I meant. Trees to him are all the same, just things to prune or chop down.

It was awful when he cut down the poplar trees. Dad asked him to because the neighbours were complaining about them keeping out the light, but I hated it. There was sawdust everywhere, and piles of logs that used to be branches, and a bitter smell of sap, like lemons. It looks bare and empty above the garden fence now, we can see right through to the back of the shops with their ugly fire escapes.

I said it looked awful, and Hedge said, 'Time comes when they has to go. There's plenty more trees.'

He doesn't care about things dying.

He used to have an old black and white dog called Bess, then he got Kelly as a pup, and Bess wasn't around any more. Mrs Potter said he shot her because she was getting old and stiff. How could he do that? Dad said it was probably kinder than taking her to the vet, because Bess wouldn't know what was going to happen. I suppose he's right, but I know Dad couldn't do a thing like that.

Hedge scares me and I hate him, but I'm not going to think about him. It's a lovely day and the war really is going to end soon, everything is all right. Swing to and fro, lean back, stare up at the blue sky that rocks gently above me —

CRASH!

It's a huge explosion. Leaves are scattering down. I've jammed my feet into the ground, I'm off the swing, running towards the house.

Mum's at the back door.

'Katie, come in, quickly!'

She stands back to let me into the kitchen then shuts the door as if it will keep danger out. Ian's under the kitchen table, pushing a model train about. He seems to think one table is as safe as another. Since the doodlebugs stopped, Mum hasn't minded where he plays. He doesn't seem bothered by the huge bang.

Mum and I both stare through the window. Smoke is rising from behind the shops. 'For goodness' sake,' she mutters. 'Not *another* new weapon.'

'I didn't hear any engine,' I tell her. 'But it might have been gliding.'

She shakes her head. 'Not that far. We've always heard them cut out.'

She's right.

Mrs Potter bursts in through the back door, looking agitated. She's wearing earth-stained rubber gloves.

'What on earth was that?' she says. 'I was weeding the path, and it came from nowhere. Not a sound, just bang, out of the blue.'

Ian looks up and frowns. 'What do you mean?' he asks.

Nobody answers.

Mum fills the kettle and sets it on the gas.

'Time for a cup of tea,' she says. 'Ian, would you like a biscuit and some milk?'

'Yes, please,' he says. He's gone back to pushing his model train about and making shunting noises, so he can't be too worried about the bang.

Mum is, though.

'Would you like to play with that in the Morrison?' she asks. 'Just for a little while?' Our kitchen table won't be much good if there's a closer explosion.

'It's too soft in the Morrison,' Ian says. 'Blankets and things. It's no good for trains.'

'There's more important things than trains,' says Mrs Potter, although Mum's giving her a warning glance. 'You get in there like your mum says.'

Ian stands up, clutching his trucks and locomotive. He's frowning. 'Why do I have to?' he asks.

'Just to keep in practice,' Mum says.

'Because it's a new sort of doodlebug?'

'Well – it might be.'

He sighs and goes off to the Morrison.

'Bless him,' says Mrs Potter.

'Go with him, Katie, there's a dear,' says Mum.

For a moment I feel almost insulted. I'm older than Ian, I want to be here with the grown-ups.

'Please,' says Mum. 'Keep him company.'

So I go and cuddle in beside Ian. His train is parked on the top of the Morrison, and he's curled up in the shelter with his blanket and Bun. When things are dangerous he's just plain scared, and that's quite sensible, really. I don't know why I'm different, but I am. I'd much rather be out there, wearing a tin hat and doing something useful, being part of it. I can't wait to be grown-up.

The rest of the day was a drag. We had another bang this afternoon, then a couple more just after Dad got home. He doesn't know what this new thing is, but he said he saw new bomb damage from the train, and the site was enormous.

Mum had promised I could have a bath. The water's not always hot enough, because we can't get as much coal for the stove as we really need. I was looking forward to it, so when she didn't want to let me go upstairs because of these new explosions, I was really fed up. But Dad said we have to trust to luck, so I'm up here, soaking luxuriously in hot water. It's deep enough so all of me is underneath it except just my toes sticking up beside the plug chain. It's still daylight and the birds are singing outside.

I slide my feet under the water, and my knees come up like small islands in a soapy sea. I drape my flannel over them.

BANG!

It's further away than the other one, but heavy and loud.

Mum's running up the stairs. She taps at the door.

'Out of there, quickly,' she says. 'Get dried and come downstairs.'

I scramble up from the bath and pull the plug out, grab a towel. That's the end of my bit of luxury.

I'm going down to the kitchen, but I look in through the dining-room door. Ian is tucked up in the Morrison and Dad's sitting on the floor beside him, reading 'The Great Big Scissor Man'. Dad's still not taken to the Morrison. He only crawls into it last thing at night when the rest of us are more or less asleep. I remember what Mum told me about the bad time he had in that other war. He never says anything about it, but I know it must have been awful, because when there's a noisy raid, his hands tremble.

Mum's listening to the radio, but as I come in, the announcer says, 'That's the end of the news.' It starts playing a cheerful tune. Mum switches it off.

'They say these things are a kind of rocket,' she says. 'They call them the V-2.'

Somehow, we can't feel scared all over again. It's just kind of depressing.

The doodlebugs were supposed to be the V-1, Victory One, the weapon that would win the war for Germany. Only it didn't. I suppose they hope this one will.

I don't know what we're going to call them. They come so fast, they can't be seen. They're not bugs. They don't doodle. They're just rockets.

'Light the blue paper and stand back,' I say like an idiot, remembering the rockets we used to have on Bonfire Night before the war. I used to get so excited, even though it was usually raining and Dad was always in a bad temper. He hated fireworks.

Perhaps that was because of the other war, too. Whatever the reason, he was useless at managing them. Catherine wheels always fell off the fence and fizzled around at our feet, or else he nailed them on too hard and they wouldn't turn, just spat and hissed, and rockets were usually a disaster. We stood them in a milk bottle, and Dad would keep striking matches until he got one to stay alight. Then he'd make a very long arm and turn his face away while he gingerly applied the flame to the firework. Sometimes the rocket would go whooshing into the sky and burst into red or green or white stars, and Mum and I cheered – Ian wasn't born then – but mostly, the whoosh didn't happen. If our rockets got out of the milk bottle at all, they tended to nose-dive into some very wet part of the garden.

These V-2 rockets can't be like that.

'They must be very big,' I say to Mum. 'As big as the doodlebugs.'

'Or even bigger,' she says. And she sighs. 'This is the beginning of a new kind of war. From now on, we'll be firing these long-distance rockets. Frontiers and defences will be useless.'

Dad comes in from reading to Ian and hears this. He shakes his head. 'I don't know what it's coming to,' he says. 'Decent wars should be fought by young men on horses. Using swords. And only if they want to.'

Mum smiles at him, but she looks sad. She takes the kettle from the stove and turns to fill it at the sink. Making tea is like the chorus of a song – it's something we all join in with, after the latest verse about whatever's happened.

'I'll have a cup later,' Dad says.

He turns away to the door, humming a bit, and I know he's going to play the piano, which is in the front room. In the winter, there's always an argument about whether we have a fire in there and sit with Dad and his piano, or in the back room where the radio is. If there's no fire in the piano room, he plays just the same, but with his coat on, and his scarf and fingerless mittens. Sometimes people stop in the street and listen, but he doesn't know about that.

CRASH!

The windows rattle, and there's a scrape and clatter as a couple of tiles fall off the roof and land on the concrete path outside.

'Come on,' Mum says wearily. 'We'd better get inside the Morrison.'

Dad has taken no notice of the explosion. From the front room, we can hear him playing the steady notes of Bach's 'Jesu, Joy of Man's Desiring'. His hands never tremble when he's playing the piano.

5

Terror

I'm letting the train window down on its leather strap, leaning out to look for Pauline as we come into her station. We get in the No Smoking compartment at the end of the third carriage if we can – all the others are Smoking, and they're really stinky. But this morning I only just caught the train, and I'm not so far along.

There she is, she's seen me, she's running along the platform. The guard's blowing his whistle, but I've got the door open for her. She's scrambling in, flopping down with her satchel and a pie dish because she made apple crumble in Domestic Science yesterday. They have to bring their own margarine and sugar because it's on ration, but there are lots of apples at the moment, so the school provides those. The DS people get to take their stuff home to eat, lucky things. I'm in the Latin group, so I don't do practical things like cooking.

Pauline must have been late like me this morning, she's out of breath and her face is bright pink. She's got orange freckles, so it looks totally hectic. Her school beret has come off as usual. She wears it skewered to her red hair with a hatpin, flat as a navy-blue pancake, but it falls off when she runs. Her mac is unbuttoned and her tie is all over the place – she's always getting into trouble for being untidy, but she doesn't care. She's not much bothered about school really. She's so busy at home, with the little ones to look after, it's a wonder she turns up at all, but she always does.

'My gran's ill,' she says. 'Someone came to tell Mum this morning. I said I'd go and see her after school – will you come? She likes a bit of company, it cheers her up.'

'As long as it's not for too long,' I say. 'I don't want Mum to worry.'

'No, we'll just pop in. She lives near

Elmer's End station. We can get off the train there, do a quick visit and be back in time for the next one.'

'OK.'

I get the later train if there's something after school like choir rehearsal, or if I miss the one that goes at ten-past four. Mum won't panic if I'm only half an hour late.

'What's the matter with your gran?' I ask.

'It's her chest,' says Pauline.

I nod, trying to look as if I understand – but trouble with your chest can be anything from a bit of a cold to pneumonia. Pauline's gran has always wheezed, but I thought it was just the smoking. She loves her cigarettes.

Pauline's gran is in bed in the small downstairs room, wheezing and coughing. She got the bed moved down when the raids started, and it's crammed in between the other furniture. She never throws anything away, and every surface is crowded with clothes, ornaments, rugs, shawls, books, old photographs and dirty teacups. The fire is out and the cold hearth is a mess of ash and cinders.

Pauline dumps her school bag on the floor and kisses the old lady, who smiles at the sight of her then goes into a fit of coughing. Her teeth are in a glass by the bed. She reaches for my hand and gives it a squeeze, still coughing, and manages to say, 'Nice to see you, pet.'

She looks very ill, but Pauline goes on being cheerful. 'I'll make a cup of tea,' she says. 'You'd like one, wouldn't you, Gran?'

Between coughs, her gran says, 'Lovely.'

The scullery is piled with dirty dishes, and the sink is half full of scummy water.

'Poor Gran!' Pauline says. 'I don't suppose she could get any coal in. I'll light the fire, we'll need some hot water. Stick the kettle on, Katie.'

She grabs the coal hod and hauls the back door open. I find some matches and light the gas. It's selfish of me to feel dismayed, but I do. I can't stay and help with all this.

Pauline lugs the full coal hod through, with sticks and newspaper tucked under the other arm. When the back boiler behind the fire has heated the water enough, she'll wash the dishes and get the place cleared up.

That's fine, I can see her gran really needs help, but Mum will be frantic if I stay any later. If only I could let her know – I go back into the room where Pauline is raking out the ash and cinders.

'There isn't a phone, is there?' I ask quietly, but she shakes her head, as I expected. Pauline's house doesn't have a phone, either. Not many people do. We're lucky – the bank said my dad had to have one so they could get in touch if they needed to.

Gran hands me a cold hot-water bottle draped in a pink vest and says, 'Could you fill that for me, dear?'

I find a saucepan under the sink and set that on the gas as well. There's a tray beside the cooker, so I wipe it and put out cups. Just two, I don't want to stay for tea. There's no bottled milk in the cupboard, just a rather sticky tin of the evaporated sort with two triangular holes punched in the top. It smells sweetish, as usual. I expect it's all right – this stuff never seems to go off. The sugar bowl is almost empty, but there's no more in the cupboard. Probably she's used up her ration.

'Thank you, dear,' Gran says when I take the tray in. She's trying to sit up.

Pauline comes to help her, thumping the pillows into a better shape. The bed smells frowsty. 'You got any clean sheets, Gran?' she asks.

'Bathroom cupboard,' says Gran with more wheezing. 'I can't manage the stairs, dear, not just now.'

'Course you can't. That's all right, I'll find them.'

The clock that's half buried under the clutter on the mantelpiece says ten to five. Pauline catches my glance at it.

'If you want to go, that's fine,' she says. 'I don't mind, honest.'

'If you're sure. It's just that—'

'I know, you said.' She clears a space on the table for me to put the tray down. 'Thanks a lot for helping.'

I've hardly helped at all, really.

'Go on,' says Pauline, shooing me like a chicken. 'See you tomorrow.'

Houses and their back gardens are slipping past the train window in the autumn

63

sunshine. I'm sorry for Pauline's gran, she's old and ill and she can't cope, but I'm glad to be out of that cramped, stuffy house. I realise how lucky I am. I think of our kitchen that's big enough for the four of us to sit round a table and the garden with fruit trees and a swing, and feel a fresh rush of love for my home. Our dining room looks a bit of a mess just now because of the Morrison in it, but we've still got the front room with the sofa and chairs and the fawn-coloured carpet and Dad's piano.

The train slides into my station. I pull the catch of the door back – and gasp. The glass has been blown out of the roof. It's lying in jagged heaps on the platform, together with the twisted and broken remains of the bars that held it up. There's been a rocket, terribly near.

I can't run on the sliding layers of broken glass, but I'm hurrying on wobbly legs towards the barrier where the ticket man is standing. I show him my season ticket and ask, 'Where did it fall?'

He jerks his thumb. 'Round the corner past the garage. Half-way up the lane.'

That's where we live.

I'm running now, out of the station entrance and down the road. People are outside their shops, sweeping up glass. It gets worse towards the corner; there's debris scattered everywhere. A bus is driving through it, very slowly. I'm out of breath, my school bag is heavy with books, but I keep running. The garage on the corner is just about standing, but it's a roofless wreck. A van is lying on its side in what used to be the workshop.

I can't see my house yet, but something terrible may be waiting. These are the last moments before I know. I slow down, but the dread makes me feel so sick that I start hurrying again. Round the corner – I don't want to look. But I have to.

Mrs Potter's house is standing, though most of its roof has gone, but ours, that was joined onto it, isn't there any more. Neither are the ones beyond it, the Thomsons', the Blacks', the Midgeleys'. The empty space seems immense. Fire engines and rescue trucks are standing in the road, and an ambulance as well. A sliced-off bit of our house's front wall still stands, with the brown velvet curtains hanging at the shattered windows, but behind it there's just emptiness.

Where is Mum? Where is Ian?

I'm making a wailing noise though I don't mean to, and coughing because of the sharpness of dust and rubble in my throat. I'm blundering across fire hoses, tripping over lumps of the stuff that was our house. The perfume of lavender comes up from the crushed bushes where the path was. I stumble round the pile of rubble where men are moving lengths of timber and heaving lumps of masonry aside. I can see part of the kitchen floor under my feet, its zig-zag-patterned lino covered with wreckage. The sink is leaning sideways on its bent pipes. The trees in the garden are shattered and broken, the swing dangles from one rope. There's a crowd of people but I can't see who they are. I'm blinded with tears and I can't think of anything, only that Mum and Ian are somewhere under the pile of rubble that was our house.

'Katie!' someone says. 'Oh, come here, pet, thank God you're all right.' I'm being clutched against Mrs Potter's apron. 'Ian's here,' she's saying, 'look, he's fine.'

He's standing beside her, and I hug him like I'll never let him go again. There's a cut on his head that's dribbling blood over his eyebrow and down the side of his face, but he's alive, he's alive. He leans close against me with his head pressed against my school mac. His hair is matted with blood.

'It needs to be seen to,' Mrs Potter says, 'there might be glass in it or something. They tried to get him in the ambulance, but he wasn't having it.'

'I was waiting for you,' Ian says, his voice muffled by the navy gabardine of my mac. 'You were late.'

'I know. I'm sorry.'

'Just as well,' says Mrs Potter. 'You wouldn't have wanted to be on that platform when the thing fell.'

Ian's clutching Mum's blue cardigan. The sight of it makes my heart jump with sudden hope.

'Did Mum give you that to look after?' I ask him.

He hugs it tighter. 'Yes. We were picking

beans and she took them in the kitchen. Then there was the bang. It threw me into the fence. Look.'

He shows me his grazed arm.

Mum would have dabbed it with iodine. It stings dreadfully, but things always heal up. She hasn't done it this time. There's no sign of its yellow-brown colour.

'Where's Mum gone?' Ian wails. 'Where is she?'

Mrs Potter looks at me with a kind of warning, then glances sideways to where the Rescue men are carefully shifting spars and lumps of masonry from the wreckage. Her message is plain. My mother is under there. The men are trying to find her.

I cram my hand over my mouth and nose and manage to push the tears away somewhere, swallow them down. I have to be tough. It may be that from now on, I'll be the only mum Ian's got. But I don't know how to be like Mum, I'm not her.

There's a firm hand on my shoulder. I turn in stupid hope, but it isn't Mum, of course. It's Hedge, with his dog at his heels. He's staring at me from his grooved brown face that never looks clean. His eyes are the colour of iodine.

'Don't you give up hope, girl,' he says to me. 'Don't you fret. We'll find her.' He turns to Ian and nods at the blue cardigan. 'That belong to your mum, son?'

'Yes.'

Hedge seems pleased.

'Kelly, here,' he says, and the dog comes to sit beside him, looking up expectantly. 'Show him the woolly, there's a good boy,' Hedge tells Ian. 'Let him get the scent of it.'

Ian doesn't argue. He holds Mum's cardigan out to Kelly, who stands up and sniffs at it carefully. He moves the tip of his tail from side to side, just a little bit.

'Come, Kelly,' says Hedge. '*Find.*' He sets off to where the men are working, with the dog loping at his heels.

He speaks to the foreman, who nods and picks up a loud-hailer. His amplified voice rings out.

'Quiet, everyone, please. We're going to put a dog in, we need to hear. Everyone quiet.'

Kelly starts to explore the wreckage, moving across it carefully. His nose is down, very close to the broken timbers and lumps of plaster and brickwork. He's holding his tail in a straight line, absolutely still. We're all watching. We can see he's working hard, but he seems terribly slow.

People are starting to mutter.

'Waste of time,' a man behind me says. 'Never find her that way. They want to keep on digging.'

The noise of people talking starts to get louder.

'QUIET!' shouts the foreman, and there is silence again. I can hear the rasp and scrabble of Kelly's claws – he's suddenly started to burrow. His tail is wagging frantically now, and he's yelping sharply.

'That's where she is,' I hear Hedge say. He moves towards the dog. 'Here, Kelly. Leave it now. Good dog.'

He bends and pats him, and the pair of them move away through the crowd.

The men are lifting away bits of wreckage from the place the dog had been digging at. I'm gripping Ian's hand so hard that he wriggles it a bit.

'Sorry,' I tell him.

'It's all right,' he says. But he's still frowning, and he rubs with his sleeve at the blood that's drying on his face, as though it itches.

'Quiet again, please!' the foreman shouts. In the silence, there's the sound of a thin cry, almost as if someone has woken up in a state of surprise.

Ian's face clears. 'It's Mum!' he says.

Mrs Potter smiles at him and puts her finger to her lips. There's been a buzz from the watching people, but we're all quiet again now. We can hear the clatter of every plank and spar tossed aside, the thud and thump of bricks and hunks of cement.

The foreman says, 'Hold it a minute.' He's stooping down. 'Keep talking to us,' we hear him say. 'We can see you, we're almost there. Stick with it, we'll have you out in a minute.'

I can't hear Mum's answer, just the faint sound of her voice.

'Perhaps she's in the Morrison,' says Ian. He's trying to be brave. 'It's safe in there, isn't it.'

'Yes,' I say. But the place where the men are digging is not where the dining room used to be. I think it was the kitchen. Or maybe she was upstairs. That's a horrible thought.

'So she'll be all right,' Ian goes on.

'She'll be fine,' I tell him. And secretly cross the fingers of the hand that isn't holding his, praying that it's true.

6

Ambulance

We're in the ambulance. Ian and I are
sitting close beside each other on the bunk
seat with a red blanket over our knees.
Ian's counting the stitches along its
edge. He's still got Mum's cardigan, but
he's put it down beside him. An ambulance
lady sits on the seat at the end. She smiles
whenever I look at her. Mum is lying
on the stretcher they slid into the
ambulance after they'd got her out of the
wreckage. She's under a red blanket, too.
Her face is filthy and one of her eyes is
blackened and swollen, but she's all right,
she's talked to us. She said she thought
she had a broken leg, but we weren't to
worry because she was going to be fine.

Then they gave her an injection to make her feel more comfortable. She hasn't said much since then.

Scary thoughts keep darting through my head. I try not to notice them, but they're hard to get rid of. *We don't have a home any more. I don't know where we'll go.* There are supposed to be Reception Centres for people who have been bombed out, but I don't know where they are or what they're like. Perhaps they'll take us to a church hall or something.

I mustn't be upset. I'm the lucky one. I'm not hurt. If I hadn't gone with Pauline to see her gran, I might have been at the station when the rocket fell.

There's netting stuck on the inside of the ambulance windows to stop the glass from blowing in if there's an explosion. It's the same on the buses, only they have a small oblong cut in the middle of each window so you can see where to get out. There isn't a clear oblong on these windows, but they're made of dark glass, so I wouldn't see much anyway. I suppose it's to stop people looking in.

I don't know what the time is. Perhaps Dad's home by now. No. *Our home isn't there.* Back from the office, I mean. He'll have walked down Station Approach like I did, knowing there's been a rocket. I don't suppose he ran – he's grown-up, he doesn't let things upset him so much. Or perhaps he does, but he'd never say. Someone might have phoned him at the bank, to tell him what had happened. I hope they did. I hope he knows we're safe.

There isn't a piano any more.

I wish I hadn't thought of that, but I can't un-think it now. All its music gone, its dark wood and ivory keys smashed and under the rubble.

My throat aches suddenly and tears are swimming in my eyes, I can't stop them. I'm trying not to make any noise, but Mum has heard me. She reaches out from her bunk. Her hand feels very cold, but her grip is strong and comforting. She's still my mum.

I'm OK again, I'm not crying. *There are more pianos*, Dad will say. Only the other day, he was telling me how the very best ones, the great, glossy concert grand pianos, are made in Germany, the country we are fighting. There must be people there who

75

are like us, sick of the war. After a minute, I tuck Mum's hand back under her blanket. She murmurs, 'Thank you, darling.' And the ambulance lady smiles at me again.

I'm in a corridor with chairs along the wall. They've given me a cup of tea and a magazine. They said Ian would be back quite soon, but Mum will have to stay in hospital. She has to have an operation. It's not just her leg, the nurse said – she's got a broken hip as well, and broken ribs.

The magazine is an old *National Geographic*, with pictures of African men paddling canoes and dancing with spears and pointy shields. There aren't any stories. But I couldn't concentrate on a story, so it doesn't matter. I'm holding Mum's blue cardigan. They told Ian to let me look after it while they saw to the wound on his head, and he handed it over without any arguing.

There are double doors with round windows in them almost opposite where I'm sitting. That's the room where Ian is. The nurse said he'd probably need stitches. It's stupid to go on staring at the doors, it won't make the waiting time any shorter. I take another look at the magazine, but it's truly boring.

I keep thinking about Hedge. I wanted to run after him when Kelly had found where Mum was, but I was holding Ian's hand and I couldn't. I feel so guilty. It's not long since I actually wished Hedge had died instead of Mr Freeman. I know why I wished it – I was angry, and I hated Hedge because he scared me. In a way, he still does. But Mr Freeman didn't have a dog. He wouldn't have come to the wreckage of our house and put a hand on my shoulder, telling me not to fret. It was Hedge who did that, and Hedge who went over to the men who were digging. And after his dog had found where Mum was, Hedge turned quietly aside and disappeared into the crowd without waiting for any thanks.

I'll say a big thank you when I see him, of course I will – but I wish I could tell him I'm sorry for what I thought about him. I can't, though. It would sound stupid.

I wish there was some way of knowing when you're being stupid.

The doors are opening again. Ian's coming out with a nurse who's holding his hand. His head is covered by a turban of white bandage that goes from his eyebrows to a tuft of hair that sticks out at the top, and underneath it his face is almost as white. He sits down beside me and picks up Mum's cardigan, holding it to his cheek while he starts to suck his thumb. He doesn't often do that now. I expect he wants Bun and his blanket, but he doesn't ask for them.

'He was a very good boy,' the nurse says. 'And your dad's here – they phoned from Reception to say he's on his way up.'

Ian and I both turn to look at the doors at the end of the corridor – and, like magic, they swing open and Dad comes though.

Ian gets off his chair and starts towards him, and Dad picks him up as if he was a toddler again, hoisting him carefully to his shoulder and holding him tight. I go to join them.

Dad gently puts a strand of hair back from my face. 'Well, Katie,' he says. 'We're all still here. That's the main thing, isn't it.'

I just nod. It's so good to feel his arm round me.

7

Afterwards

A year's gone by. Pauline and I are sitting on the grass on the common, eating apples. They're from a tree in our garden that bloomed again this spring. I go back there to look at the garden sometimes, though I didn't at first. The house is getting rebuilt, but it won't be ready for months yet. We're in a bungalow on Park Road for now. It's a bit crowded, but it's good for Mum because there aren't any stairs. She gets around OK, but her hip still hurts sometimes.

It's warm and sunny, but this is the beginning of September. We start school again next week.

'How's your gran?' I ask.

'OK,' says Pauline. 'She likes it in the home. We didn't think she would, but she says she enjoys the company.'

The war is over now. It ended a couple of months ago. Mum and Dad and Ian and I went to London to see the celebrations. Such a lot of light! All the street lamps were on and the shop windows were lit up, and two searchlights made the form of a V for Victory in the sky. It was funny to see them perfectly still like that, not moving about in search of planes. There were masses of fireworks. Ian was scared at first, and Dad didn't like them much, either, but we found a doorway where rocket sticks couldn't fall on our heads, and watched from there. I've never seen such crowds. As we got near Trafalgar Square, I thought I was going to be squashed flat. Ian was all right, he was on Dad's shoulders.

'We had a letter from Dad yesterday,' Pauline says as if she'd picked up my thoughts. 'He's got his Demob papers – he'll be coming home next month.'

'That's terrific.'

'Great, isn't it.' She's smiling all over her freckled face. 'Mum asked at the garage, and they said he can have his job back. There'll be a lot more cars about soon, because the factories will start making them again.'

The sun filters through the leaves above us. I lie back, munching the last of my apple. I can't say this to Pauline, but I kind of miss the war. Knowing there's no danger any more makes everything seem a bit flat. The biggest thing in our lives has disappeared, and nothing else has taken its place. Peace hasn't made any real difference yet, except the fighting's stopped. Food is still rationed and the shops are still empty. I don't mean I'm wishing for people to be killed and houses destroyed and little kids hurt – of course not. But there was a kind of dreadful excitement about wartime, and that's gone.

The thought of it makes me feel restless.

'Shall we go and look at our tree?' I suggest. I don't know if Pauline will agree. We're nearly grown-up now, perhaps we don't climb trees any more. But she's scrambling to her feet.

'Yeah, let's,' she says.

The tree is standing there, the same as ever. Its leaves are starting to turn yellow in the late summer sunshine, and its trunk is smooth and grey. I look up at the place above me where the big branch grows out sideways, and think of sitting there with my feet dangling in the air.

'Go on,' says Pauline.

So I pull myself up to the easy place where the trunk divides, and feel the solid strength of the tree under my hands. The climb is the same as ever – I think I could do it blindfold. The bark has its resin-sharp smell, the leaves flicker in the sun. Pauline has settled in her usual place – looking down, I can see her red hair.

There is nothing in the sky above us except the swooping, twittering swallows. They're restless, too. They're always like that at this time of year, starting to think about the long journey ahead of them.

I hope they'll be safe.

Glossary

Air raid   A form of attack where bombs are dropped from aircraft onto enemy towns.

Anderson shelter   A small arch of corrugated steel designed to be partly buried in people's gardens to act as a shelter during air raids.

Anti-aircraft guns   Guns positioned on the ground used to target enemy aircraft.

Barrage balloons   Huge balloons designed to defend towns, cities and key targets from air attack. The balloons were secured with steel cables and used to deter low-flying enemy planes.

Blackout curtains   Thick, heavy curtains intended to stop house lights from attracting the attention of enemy pilots during an air raid.

Coal hod   A container used to carry coal.

Debris   The remains of something that has been destroyed or broken up.

Demob (Demobilisation)   The release of soldiers from military service.

Doodlebug A name for the V-1 bomb.

Encampment   A temporary camp built by an army for soldiers to live in.

Foreman   A person who gives orders to workers.

Frontier   The border around a country.

Gabardine Tightly woven material usually used for outdoor clothing.

Hurricane lamp   An oil lamp with a glass covering to prevent the flame from being blown out.

Iodine   An antiseptic used on a wound to stop bacteria from spreading.

Lino (Linoleum)   A plastic-like floor covering.

Masonry   Building materials made from stone, brick or concrete.

Morrison shelter An air-raid shelter made up of a metal table with wire mesh sides designed to be used indoors.

Munitions   Military equipment and supplies.

Rationing   Limiting the amount of food given to people when food is scarce.

Scullery   A small room next to the kitchen where pots and pans are scrubbed and stored.

Shrapnel   Fragments of metal that fly off a bomb when it explodes.

Spar An iron or wooden pole or rod.

Swastika   The shape used as the symbol of Nazi Germany.

Timber   Wood cut and prepared for use as building material.

V-1   A bomb invented by the Germans in World War II that had wings and flew on its own: used especially to attack London.

V-2   A rocket-powered missile invented by the Germans in World War II: used especially to attack London.

Historical Note

Between September 1940 and May 1941, London and the surrounding areas experienced almost nightly bomb raids from German planes. This was known as the 'Blitz' – short for the German word *Blitzkrieg*, meaning 'lightning war'. During these nine months over a million houses were damaged or destroyed and one in six Londoners were made homeless. People's daily routines and ways of life were changed completely, although in a sense they were replaced by another routine; one of blackouts, fire watching, air-raid sirens and nights spent in shelters.

The government provided households with Anderson shelters to dig into their gardens. These were made from an arch of corrugated steel, which was then covered in a thick layer of earth for protection. People would often plant vegetables on top, as food was rationed. Although Londoners were supposed to sleep in the shelters every night, some people preferred to risk staying in their homes. The shelters were cold, cramped and dark, and they often flooded.

After a particularly devastating raid on London on the night of 10th May 1941 there was a lull from the nightly drone of the bombers. For nearly three years there was almost no bombing at all. To some degree, life went back to normal, and people could return to sleeping in their homes at night. However, this wasn't to last.

In the summer of 1944 a new kind of bomb started hitting the capital. The V-1 was the first of Hitler's secret weapons that he promised would win Germany the war. The V stood for *Vergeltungswaffe*, the German word for 'revenge weapon'. However Londoners soon came up with a name of their own: the 'buzz bomb' or 'doodlebug', after the characteristic insect-like buzzing sound of its engine.

The V-1 was like nothing that had come before and was capable of bombing targets at very long distances. It was basically a small, pilotless aircraft, with no navigational system. The doodlebug was simply launched in the direction of its target from a makeshift ramp. It would fly until its engine ran out of fuel; then come crashing down to earth, exploding as it hit the ground. Although the noise of the doodlebugs flying overhead was bad enough, what people dreaded most was the noise of an engine cutting out. When this happened you knew you were in trouble. All you could do was dive for cover and hope the rocket would glide for a bit before it fell.

As the V-1s were launched in the daytime, when many people were on the streets, they caused large numbers of casualties. Around 100 of the bombs were launched towards London every day from sites on the French and the Dutch coasts. Around half of these reached Greater London, whilst others fell over the south east of England.

There were ways of stopping the bombs, but any action had to be taken before the V-1s reached London and away from populated areas. Fighter pilots learned new tricks to destroy the bombs; they found that they could fly alongside the weapon and tip over one of its wings so that it was knocked off course. A combination of RAF aircraft, barrage balloons and anti-aircraft guns succeeded in bringing down nearly two-fifths of V-1s. However London was soon to face an even more terrifying weapon – one that came without warning and could not be defended against.

When the first V-2 rocket made its attack on September 8 1944, the explosion could be heard throughout London. The strange new explosions continued over the weeks to follow. At first no one really knew what had caused the blasts and officials told the public that the incidents were gas mains explosions.

It gradually became apparent that this was a new secret weapon. A rocket that flew faster than the speed of sound and was pretty much invisible after it had been fired. The first people on the ground knew of the V-2 was when it exploded. Because of this, the V-2 inspired even more terror than previous weapons. At least with the doodlebug people had a chance to take shelter under a table or in a doorway. Many Londoners confessed they were much more scared of the V-2 attacks than they had been when bombs were raining down on them during the Blitz.

The destruction of central London was so severe that the government decided to use false information to get the Germans to change their target. The government made the Germans think that it had moved its headquarters to the south east of London to escape the V-2 attacks. This tactic had some success; the Germans started to concentrate their attacks on this new area and central London received far fewer hits.

The V-2 attacks only came to an end as the Allies advanced across western Europe and took over the launch sites. Although the V-2 rocket did not win the war for Hitler, it was the most sophisticated weapon of World War II and is the forerunner of modern-day missiles.

Map of England and
Northern Europe

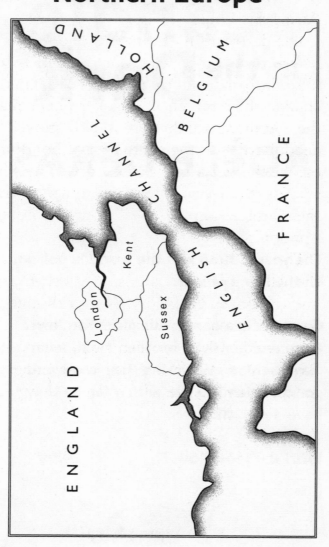

A Candle in the Dark

ADÈLE GERAS

The year is 1938 and the world is poised on the brink of war...

Germany is a dangerous place for Jews. Clara and her little brother, Maxi, must leave behind everything they know and go to England to live with a family they have never met.

ISBN 0-7136-7454-7   £4.99

CASTING THE GODS ADRIFT

GERALDINE McCAUGHREAN

The year is 1351 BC and a new pharaoh is ruling Egypt...

When Tutmose and his family arrive in Pharaoh Akhenaten's new city, they are delighted to be taken under the ruler's wing. But the pharaoh's strange ideas about religion will change life for them all...

ISBN 0-7136-7455-5

£4.99

ACROSS THE
ROMAN
WALL

THERESA BRESLIN

The year is 397 AD and life in Roman Britain is getting dangerous...

Marinetta is a Briton, Lucius is the nephew of a Roman official. When they first meet they hate each other. But when marauders cross Hadrian's Wall they are forced to work together.

ISBN 0-7136-7456-3   **£4.99**

MISSION TO MARATHON

GEOFFREY TREASE

The year is 490 BC and Persian forces are invading Greece...

When news reaches Athens that Persian warships are about to land at Marathon, Philip is sent on a mission — to cross the mountains and warn his family of the danger. The race is on ... will he get there in time?

ISBN 0-7136-7677-9   **£4.99**

flash backs

A GHOST-LIGHT IN THE ATTIC

PAT THOMSON

These are the 1650s and England is in
a state of civil war...

When Elinor Bassingbourn steps out of a
17th-century painting, Tom and Bridget are
terrified. But Elinor needs their help, so they
follow her back in time on an exciting,
terrifying adventure.

ISBN 0-7136-7453-9   £4.99